D1109203

ITSY BITSY SPIDER

Retold by STEVEN ANDERSON

Illustrated by TIM PALIN

CANTATA
LEARNING

MANKATO, MINNESOTA

WWW.CANTATALEARNING.COM

CANTATA
LEARNING
MANKATO, MINNESOTA

Published by Cantata Learning
1710 Roe Crest Drive
North Mankato, MN 56003
www.cantatalearning.com

Copyright © 2016 Cantata Learning

All rights reserved. No part of this publication may be reproduced
in any form without written permission from the publisher.

Library of Congress Control Number: 2014957026
978-1-63290-282-5 (hardcover/CD)
978-1-63290-434-8 (paperback/CD)
978-1-63290-476-8 (paperback)

Itsy Bitsy Spider by Steven Anderson
Illustrated by Tim Palin

Book design, Tim Palin Creative
Editorial direction, Flat Sole Studio
Executive musical production and direction, Elizabeth Draper
Music arranged and produced by Steven C Music

Printed in the United States of America.

VISIT
WWW.CANTATALEARNING.COM/ACCESS-OUR-MUSIC
TO SING ALONG TO THE SONG

Move your hands like

a spider as you sing this song!

Now turn this page, and sing along.

The **itsy bitsy** spider
climbed up the **waterspout**.

Down came the rain
and washed the spider out.

Out came the sun
and dried up all the rain.

And the itsy bitsy spider
climbed up the spout again.

The itsy bitsy spider
climbed up the waterspout.

Down came the rain
and washed the spider out.

Out came the sun
and dried up all the rain.

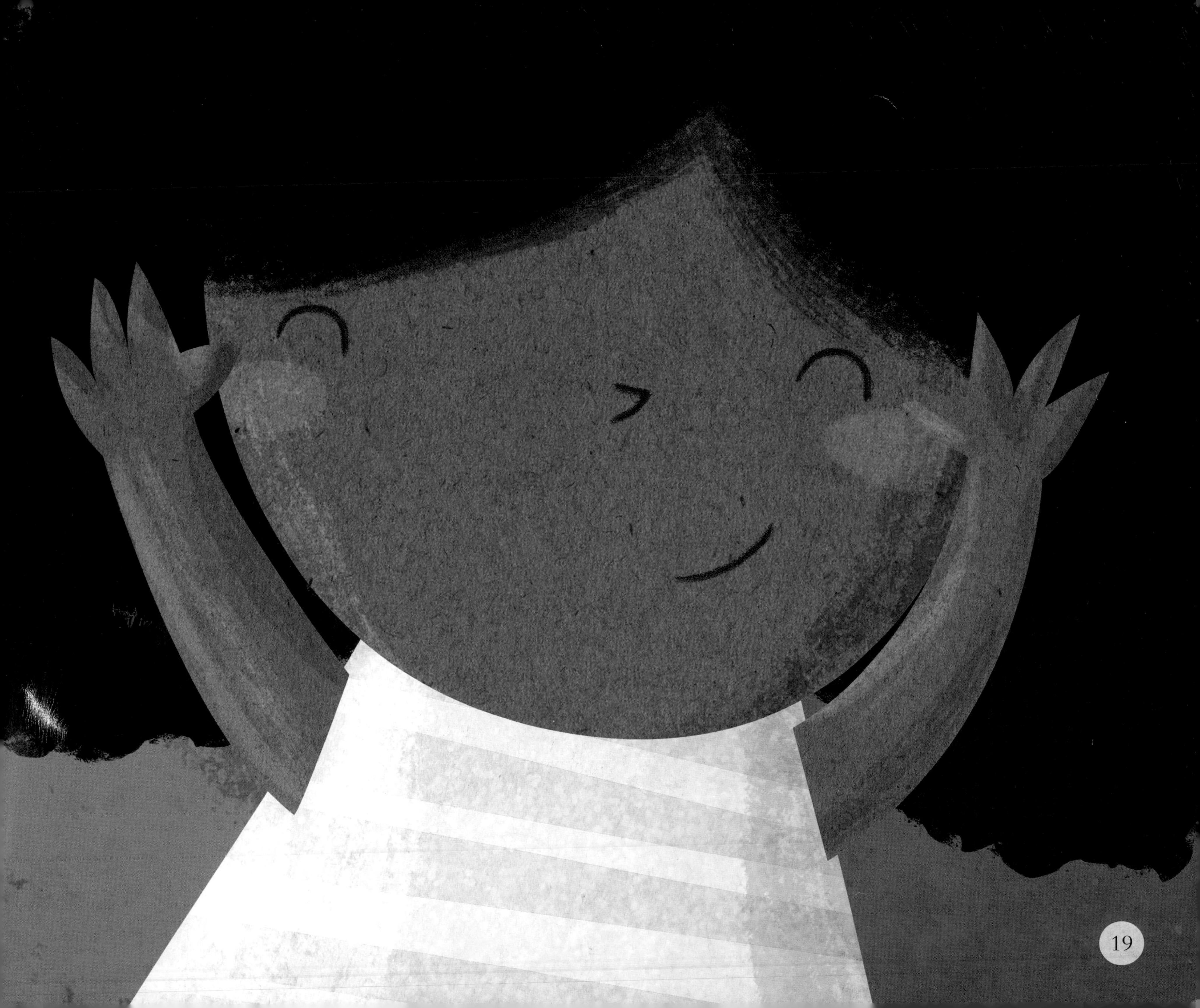

And the itsy bitsy spider
climbed up the spout again.

SONG LYRICS
Itsy Bitsy Spider

The itsy bitsy spider
climbed up the waterspout.

Down came the rain
and washed the spider out.

Out came the sun
and dried up all the rain.

And the itsy bitsy spider
climbed up the spout again.

The itsy bitsy spider
climbed up the waterspout.

Down came the rain
and washed the spider out.

Out came the sun
and dried up all the rain.

And the itsy bitsy spider
climbed up the spout again.

Itsy Bitsy Spider

Americana
Steven C Music

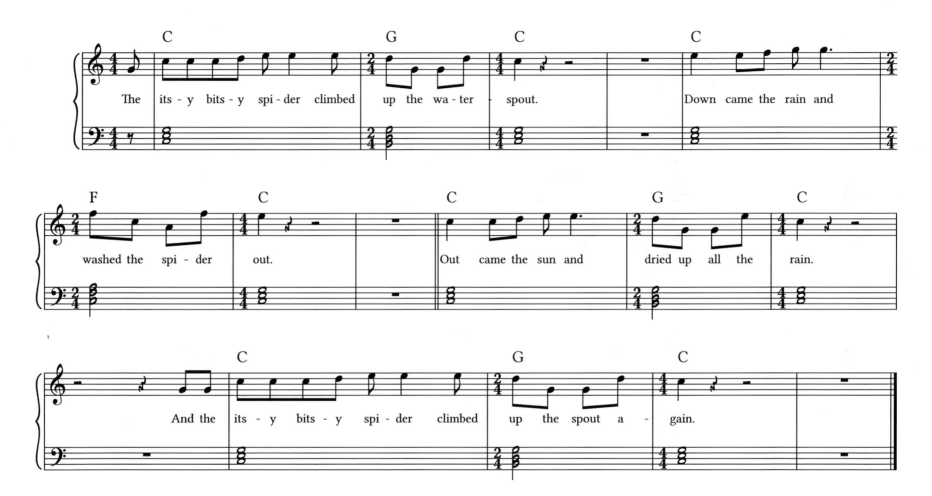

MUSIC AVAILABLE AT
WWW.CANTATALEARNING.COM/ACCESS-OUR-MUSIC

GLOSSARY

isty bitsy—very small

waterspout—a pipe that runs along the side of a building to help keep water off the roof

GUIDED READING ACTIVITIES

1. In three sentences or less, summarize what happens to the spider in this story.

2. Sing Itsy Bitsy Spider. Pretend your hands are the spider as you sing.

3. Have you ever seen a spider? What did it look like? What was it doing? Was it climbing up something? Draw a picture to tell the story of the spider you saw.

TO LEARN MORE

Cronin, Doreen. *Diary of a Spider*. New York: HarperCollins, 2013.

Emberley, Rebecca. *Itsy Bitsy Spider*. Pasadena, CA: Two Little Birds Books, 2013.

Reasoner, Charles. *Itsy Bitsy Spider*. Mankato, MN: Picture Window Books, 2013.

Smith, Sian. *Spiders*. Chicago: Raintree, 2013.